First published in Great Britain in 2019 by Pat-a-Cake
Copyright © Hodder & Stoughton Limited 2019. All rights reserved
Pat-a-Cake is a registered trade mark of Hodder & Stoughton Limited
ISBN: 978 1 52638 207 8 • 10 9 8 7 6 5 4 3 2 1
Pat-a-Cake, an imprint of Hachette Children's Group,
Part of Hodder & Stoughton Limited
Carmelite House, 50 Victoria Embankment, London EC4Y 0DZ
An Hachette UK Company
www.hachette.co.uk • www.hachettechildrens.co.uk
Printed in China

The Little Mermaid

Retold by Ronne Randall
Illustrated by Junissa Bianda

Little Mermaid

beach

ship

Sea Witch

potion

Prince

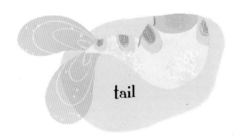

tail

legs

palace gardens

Once there was a Little Mermaid who lived under the sea.
She loved to sing. Her voice was as clear and bright as silver bells.

The Little Mermaid was happy in her home beneath the waves. But she longed to know what life was like on land.

"One day, you will find out," her friends said.

On her sixteenth birthday, the Little Mermaid was allowed
to swim up to the surface. She looked around in wonder.
There was so much light – the world was so bright!

Nearby, she saw a big ship. On the deck stood a handsome
young Prince. The Little Mermaid was very curious about him
and where he had come from.

Suddenly, the sky turned deep, dark blue. Thunder boomed and lightning crackled. The big ship shuddered and shook and rocked and rolled. The Prince stumbled and tumbled into the water.

"I have to help him!" said the Little Mermaid. She swam through the rolling waves and found the Prince.

The Little Mermaid took the Prince back to the safety of the beach. She sang to him until he opened his eyes.

The Little Mermaid wanted to tell the Prince who she was, but then, out of the corner of her eye, she spotted some people coming along the beach. She didn't want to be seen, so she slid into the sea with a swish and a flick of her tail.

Back at home, the Little Mermaid told her friends about the Prince. "I wish we could get to know him," she told them, "but how? I have a tail and cannot walk on dry land."

"Well, maybe the Sea Witch can help," said her best friend. "We will take you to see her."

The Sea Witch gave the Little Mermaid a tiny bottle.
"Drink this tonight," she said. "When you wake up tomorrow
morning, you will have legs. But you will lose your lovely voice."

The Little Mermaid looked sad because she loved to sing, but the Sea Witch spoke again.

"There is only one way to get your voice back," she said. "If the Prince says he loves you, it will come back."

That night, the Little Mermaid swam up to the shore. She drank the potion, then fell asleep on the smooth sand. In the morning, she had two legs instead of a tail.

She tried to walk, but her new legs were so shaky and achy that she fell over.

Someone gently helped her up. It was the Prince! "You are the girl who saved me in the storm!" he said. "I have been looking everywhere for you."

The Little Mermaid smiled, but she could not say a word. Her lovely voice was gone.

The Prince realised the Little Mermaid had nowhere to stay, so he took her back to the palace, where she was given fine clothes, books and her own rooms.

Over the next few weeks and months, she and the Prince went for long walks in the palace gardens. The Little Mermaid loved exploring and seeing all the amazing flowers and birds.

The Prince had a problem and he wanted to ask the Little Mermaid for some advice.

"My father wants me to marry a Princess from another kingdom," he said. "Do you think I should?"

The Little Mermaid shook her head and two big tears rolled down her cheeks.

"Oh, please don't cry!" said the Prince. "I don't care that you can't talk. I would rather marry you than a Princess I have never met. I love you!"

All at once the Little Mermaid's tears disappeared, and she broke into a sunny smile.

"And I love you!" she said, in a voice as bright and clear as silver bells.

The Prince and the Little Mermaid would be together for ever. The Little Mermaid looked out to sea. In the distance, she could see her friends, who were waving joyfully. They knew their friend would always be happy living on dry land with the Prince.

And she was!

Spot the Difference

Can you spot five differences between these pictures?

Mermaid Match

Can you find each mermaid a shell to match their tail?
Can you name the colours?